CHOOSE YOUR OWN ADVENTURE®

Kids Love Reading
Choose Your Own Adventure®!

"I like the way you can choose the way the story goes."
Beckett Kahn, age 7

"If you don't read this book, you'll get payback."
Amy Cook, age 8½

"I thought this book was funny.
I think younger and older kids will like it."
Tessa Jernigan, age 6½

"This is fun reading. Once you go in to have an
adventure, you may never come out."
Jude Fidel, age 7

Illustrated by Keith Newton
Book design by Stacey Boyd, Big Eyedea Visual Design
For information regarding permission, write to:

CHOOSECO

P.O. Box 46, Waitsfield, Vermont 05673
www.cyoa.com

A DRAGONLARK BOOK

Publisher's Cataloging-In-Publication Data
Names: Montgomery, Anson. | Newton, Keith (Illustrator at Chooseco LLC), illustrator.
Title: Your grandparents are spies / by Anson Montgomery ; illustrated by Keith Newton.
Other Titles: Choose your own adventure. Dragonlarks.
Description: Waitsfield, Vermont : Chooseco, [2016] | Summary: Your grandparents aren't the type to hide behind the newspaper or fall asleep in an armchair. In fact, they are the most fun people you know. But how well do you really know your grandparents? A man with a briefcase and a scar on his face is watching your every move, and you overhear a very surprising conversation. If your grandparents were also top-secret spies on a dangerous mission, can they still babysit you?! You choose what happens next.
Identifiers: ISBN 1937133516 | ISBN 9781937133511
Subjects: LCSH: Grandparents—Juvenile fiction. | Spies—Juvenile fiction. | CYAC: Grandparents—Fiction. | Spies—Fiction. | LCGFT: Spy fiction. | Choose-your-own stories.
Classification: LCC PZ7.M7639 Yos 2016 | DDC [Fic]—dc23

Published simultaneously in the United States and Canada

Printed in Malaysia

12 11 10 9 8 7 6 5 4 3

CHOOSE YOUR OWN ADVENTURE®

YOUR GRANDPARENTS ARE SPIES

A DRAGONLARK BOOK

This book is dedicated to all grandparents,
but especially to Chini, Shanny, Annie, Boca, and Nana.

READ THIS FIRST!!!

WATCH OUT!
THIS BOOK IS DIFFERENT
from every book you've ever read.

Do not read this book from the first page through to the last page.
Instead, start on page 1 and read until you come to your first choice. Then turn to the page shown and see what happens.

When you come to the end of a story, you can go back and start again.
Every choice leads to a new adventure.

Good luck!

You wake up on a normal Saturday morning. Something feels different. Your room is very messy, with a pile of clothes in the corner. That's normal. But why didn't Mom ask you to clean it up?

Then you remember.

Dad and Mom are away for a "romantic trip to the cabin by the lake," so Grandma and Grandpa are taking care of you and your little brother, George, and your big sister, Zelda, for the whole weekend. Friday night was okay. You all stayed up later than usual to watch the new *Action Guardians of Tolbolt* movie. George was pretty scared by all the robot battles in the movie, so you had to sit by his bed last night until he fell asleep.

Turn to the next page.

You get dressed and go downstairs. Normally you are the first one up in the whole house. You usually wake up at dawn. Everyone else likes to sleep in, even Mom and Dad. Today you hear someone in the kitchen. You recognize your grandparents' voices, talking in hushed tones.

"…we can't let the kids know!" Grandma whispers.

"I know dear, but how will we hide it from them?" Grandpa responds.

"I have a plan," Grandma says, giving a muffled laugh at the end. "It will be perfect!"

Turn to page 4.

You don't mean to eavesdrop. You walk into the kitchen and say, "Good morning, Grandma and Grandpa. It's nice to have someone else awake with me."

Both of them look up at you quickly. Then they look down at their bowls of yogurt, oatmeal, and fruit. They look like they were caught doing something. Then they both smile at you and say, "Good morning!" at the same time.

"Are you hungry?" Grandma asks. "I could make you some pancakes or some eggs."

"I'll just have cereal," you say, rubbing the sleepies out of your eyes and yawning.

"We have a question to ask you," Grandpa says as you walk to the fridge for the milk.

"Okay," you say as you pour the cereal into a bowl. A card falls out with the cereal. The card is a coupon for more Crunchy Health Pops.

This one is Mom's favorite. It isn't bad but you really wanted the Lava Chocolate Castle Bombs. You had it at your friends Allie and Tarik's house once.

Go on to the next page.

The chocolate-covered castles explode with red lava sugar when you bite into them.

"What do you want to do most in the world?" Grandma asks before adding, "After chores, of course. Your dad has a lot of projects for us to do today."

Turn to the next page.

"Most in the world?"

You *just* asked your parents if you could go to the new Mega Zip-Line Nature Exploration Park. One of the zip-lines flies you over a 300-foot deep river gorge.

Your parents said, "absolutely not." The Mega Zip-Line Nature Exploration Park was: too dangerous, too expensive, and too far away. "But it's educational! You can learn about nature!" you told them. George and Zelda wanted to go. It was three against two, but your parents have the "veto" power.

Maybe you should just ask to go to the moon? You love the idea of being on the moon, looking at the stars and jumping six times as high as you can on Earth! Maybe there is something else that you haven't even thought of yet. You think for a minute and then make your choice.

If you tell your grandparents that your best day ever would be to go zip-lining, turn to page 8.

If you make a joke and ask to go to the moon just to see what they say, turn to page 14.

"If I could go *anywhere*, I'd go zip-lining!" you say.

Your grandma looks at your grandpa and they shake their heads.

"Maybe when you are older," Grandpa says.

"Okay," you mumble. For a moment you thought they really might take you zip-lining. "I guess I'll just go over to Allie and Tarik's house."

"Not before you clean up your room," Grandma says. "Your dad was very clear about that!"

By the time you finish cleaning your room, it is late enough that your friends will be awake. You have a fun time with your friends, and then you go home to do chores with your brother and sister and grandparents for the rest of the day.

You do all the yard work, and then it's time to clean the basement. There is a HUGE spider under one of the boxes. Grandma takes the spider outside on a piece of paper. Grandpa says he is "too tired to go out for dinner!" and Grandma says she is "too tired to cook!" You order delivery Chinese food.

Turn to page 10.

You love the dumplings, so dinner is okay.

Then Grandpa says you "have to get a good night's sleep" because of all the stuff you have to do tomorrow. He wants you to go to bed at 8:30 PM on a Saturday night! That might be okay for George, since he's little, but not for you! Grandpa says Zelda can stay up until 9:00, but that's it. They don't budge. It's still light outside when you get in bed, but you are so tired you fall asleep easily.

"Wake up!" someone says, gently shaking your shoulder. You blink awake. There are very bright lights on.

"What? Huh?" you mumble. "It's too early!" You grab the covers and turn over but a hand draws them back firmly.

"Get up! We have a lot to do today!" You look up to see your grandfather staring down at you. He is wearing a black turtleneck and black pants. He pulls on a white and red one-piece track suit instead of a coat. Your grandma is waving a bundle towards you. "Come on!" she says. "We're burning daylight."

Go on to the next page.

You get up and get dressed in the clothes she presses into your hands.

George and Zelda are already in the minivan when you hop in. Wow! There are computer screens everywhere! Grandma hands you a quinoa-flavored breakfast bar. Grandpa opens a folder and pulls out four big glossy photos of a man wearing a trench coat, a hat, and sunglasses. The man holds a briefcase. The photo is blurry, but you can see that he has blond hair and a big scar on his cheek in the shape of a letter S.

"What's going on?" George asks, a whine creeping into his voice.

Grandpa backs the car out of the driveway in a spray of gravel, and Grandma turns around in her seat to face you. "We need your help!" she says. "The man in the photo stole something, and we need to get that briefcase back before he opens it. Watch the briefing video on the screens, and tell us if you see anything that might help us with the case."

Turn to page 13.

"*Welcome to Mega Zip-Line Nature Exploration Park,*" an announcer says. The video shows an overhead shot of the new park. It reminds you of the beginning of a disaster movie. "*Only here will you find the perfect blend of history, nature, and thrills!*"

Turn to page 21.

Grandpa gives a low whistle when you tell him you want to go to the moon.

"We did say 'anything'!" Grandma tells him.

"The kid asks for the moon, so we'll deliver the moon!" Grandpa mutters as he leaves the room.

Your grandparents spend all afternoon on the phone. Grandma mentions "calling in the favor from the Helsinki job" and Grandpa makes the call. When he hangs up, he gives a whoop of delight.

"Straight to the moon, Alice!" Grandpa laughs.

You tell your brother and sister.

"Clearly, we're not *really* going to the moon," Zelda says in a know-it-all voice. George runs around the room making blast-off noises with his model airplane.

"Who knows?" you say. "Grandma and Grandpa spent a lot of time making this happen. It will be cool."

Turn to page 17.

"Folks, we have a situation that has developed at the Space Center in Florida, and we don't have time to drop you off. A wildfire on our testing island has gotten out of control, and the crew needs to be rescued. This is the only plane that can help!" You look at your grandparents, but they seem as confused as you are.

The captain continues, "I'll be flying at maximum speed, and I will have to make the landing at a steep pitch. It will get bumpy, very bumpy. If you don't want to come to Florida with us, you can use the escape pod in the back. You'll land safely down below, and the Space Center crew will pick you up."

What should you do? Helping to save people sounds exciting, but also scary. So does using the escape pod.

If you choose to use the escape pod, turn to page 45.

If you decide to go with the plane on its rescue mission, turn to page 52.

Grandma and Grandpa wake you all up at 3:30 AM the next morning. This is *not* cool! Grandpa is wearing weird-looking glasses. He tells you that they are his night-vision goggles. Grandma tucks you into your seat in the minivan with a pillow and a soft blanket. You fall back asleep quickly.

Turn to the next page.

When you wake up, you've reached the gates of the Space Center. The guard calls his boss and then hands each of you a laminated badge. Your grandparents lead the way to a room filled with astronauts and scientists.

"My name is Claire Donnelli. I'm the director of the Space Center. We are honored you are here today!"

"We're the ones who are honored," Grandma says.

"We know what you did for us in Helsinki!" Claire says to your grandparents. "Benedict will show you around. He's one of our top astronauts. Do you want to go up in our jet or get suited up and do a practice space walk in our underwater training facility?"

"I thought we were going to the moon! Not just on a plane or to the pool!" George says, right to Claire.

"This is like no other plane ride, and the pool is the closest thing to outer space on Earth."

If you choose to take a ride in the weightless jet, turn to page 20.

If you decide that the underwater space walk simulator sounds better, turn to page 62.

You tell Claire you want to go on the weightless jet ride. Claire introduces you to Benedict, and he shakes your hand seriously. He's tall and very fit.

"So you want to ride in the Vomit Comet," he says. "First I'll show you around a bit."

"What's a Vomit Comet?" George asks Benedict.

"That's what they nicknamed the jet we use to make you feel weightless," Benedict answers, "and people sometimes get sick when it goes into a full dive. No one has to ride in it if they don't want to."

"George is afraid of the Vomit Comet," Zelda whispers loudly to you.

George glares at Zelda and whispers back, "Am not, I just don't like barf! Yuck!"

Turn to page 25.

You watch the video about the park and learn you are about to see one of the longest zip-lines in the world: over two miles. Your stomach churns. George clutches your arm and whimpers. You pat him and he quiets down.

As the video ends, the car stops and you look out.

You are at the entrance to the Mega Zip-Line Nature Exploration Park. Grandpa hops out, throws the car keys to one of the men dressed as explorers, and hustles you out. "Let's go!"

Turn to page 23.

A young woman with a clipboard comes up to greet you. "We lost sight of the 'target' about an hour ago. He was last seen going into the Geo-Line area," she says to Grandma.

"Thanks, Miss Sheridan," Grandma says and turns to you, George, and Zelda. "We have to hurry!"

"After an hour, he may have left the Geo-Line," Grandpa says. "Maybe we should go to the Animal-Line instead? What do you kids think?"

The Geo-Line is the zip-line over the 300-foot river gorge. It looked amazing but scary in the video. The Animal-Line is closer to the ground. It zips over island preserves at the bottom of the gorge that are home to monkeys, goats, and mountain lions. Which should you choose?

If you decide to look for your "target" in the Animal-Line area, turn to page 31.

If you choose to follow the man to the Geo-Line, turn to page 42.

Benedict leads your family around the Space Center. You visit the underwater practice pool. You all watch while a team of astronauts (or aqua-nauts) works on a module. It looks really cool, with lots of shiny metal parts and cables.

"What are they building?" you ask Benedict.

"It's a new garden module for the space station," he replies. "They grow most of their own fresh food up there now."

Turn to page 27.

"Time for the Vomit Comet, let's go suit up!" Benedict says.

You, Zelda, George, and your grandparents board the small plane wearing bright purple jumpsuits with all sorts of straps and pockets. You are excited, but also a little afraid. You don't want to get sick.

"Will you hold my hand, Grandma?" George asks, and you wish she would hold your hand too.

"Buckle up!" Grandpa yells, and you strap yourself into the seat with all four seatbelts.

WHOOOOOSH!

The plane jumps forward, and you get pushed into the back of your seat.

You have been on a plane before when you went on vacation, but this is completely different. You are moving straight up, very fast. You fly through the clouds and beyond. The sun is shining and you can see all the clouds below you glinting bright white.

After a few minutes, you hear the captain's voice over the intercom. "Get ready for the dive!" she says.

Turn to the next page.

You watch out of your window as the plane flattens out before tipping straight down!

Your stomach flutters as your body tells you that you are falling. It feels so weird! Even roller coasters aren't like this.

"You can unbuckle if you want," the captain says.

With four clicks, you are suddenly floating in the air. You grin over at your brother and sister, and they grin back. Grandma floats over and gives you a high five.

"Strap back in, folks," the captain tells you. "We're about to pull out of the dive."

You quickly buckle yourself back up. You can't believe you just flew in the air!

The captain takes you on five more dives. You, Zelda, and George bounce off the padded walls of the plane and do flips in mid-air. Grandpa just floats with his arms and legs spread out, but Grandma uses her arms and legs to push off and zip from wall to wall.

Mid-drop, the captain comes on the intercom again, and this time she sounds worried.

Turn to page 16.

"I'm sure that the 'target' has probably finished with the Geo-Line area by now," you tell the others. "Let's check out the Animal-Line!"

Turn to the next page.

Zipping from island to island is really fun! You are way up in the air, riding a thin metal cable. You are close enough to the water and the ground that it is not too scary. Even George is having a great time.

Goats jump from rock to rock as you pass overhead. Next up is Monkey Island! Most of the animals in the park are local animals, including the mountain lions, but the monkeys were rescued from a zoo that had to close.

"There's a baby!" George shouts, pointing at a baby monkey in the tree right next to you.

"Oh! She's so cute," Zelda says as the baby monkey hangs there staring at your family. Grandpa waves and the baby monkey scampers off to play.

Grandma is on the far side of the platform, sitting next to an adult monkey. It looks like Grandma is whispering something to the monkey.

"Grandma!" you whisper-shout. "Watch out!"

Grandma looks down at the monkey. It gives a nod and climbs away to the trunk of the tree and then down to the ground.

Turn to page 35.

"Ma'am, be careful, and don't feed the monkeys," says a woman wearing a safari hat and a badge.

"Oh, don't worry, young lady. I know what I'm doing. Talk to your boss and she'll tell you about the Special Agent Protocols," Grandma says, nicely but firmly. "Come on, let's go!" Grandma says to you.

"I'm hungry," George says.

"Me too," Zelda agrees.

"Good idea, kids!" Grandpa says. "Let's go to The Lion Bistro. I've heard that they make amazing waffles with whipped cream, berries, and bananas, covered in real Vermont maple syrup."

From the platform, you zip-line to the restaurant. You hurry to a table and order huge breakfasts.

"Wow, these waffles are good!" Zelda says around a huge mouthful.

"Mmm-hmm," you mumble in agreement.

"Look what Grandpa has!" George says, pointing.

Turn to page 37.

You turn around and see Grandpa holding three big stuffed animals. There is a baby monkey, a baby mountain lion, and a baby goat.

"I want the monkey!" George yells. "Please!"

"Maybe these are for your grandmother," your grandpa says with a wink.

Grandma looks at you and says, "Sweetie, your face is covered in syrup! Wash up first."

"Okay," you say, and you race from the table.

A waiter tells you where the bathroom is, and you are walking through the courtyard of tables when you see the "target"! The man with the briefcase is looking across the big moat to where the mountain lions live. The briefcase is sitting on the ground behind him. He is busy taking pictures with his camera, so you might be able to sneak up and grab the briefcase. But maybe you should go back and tell Grandma and Grandpa?

If you choose to try and grab the briefcase while the man is distracted, turn to page 38.

If you decide that the best thing is to go tell your family, turn to page 60.

You walk up slowly to the briefcase. You definitely recognize the man from the photo! He is so busy taking pictures of the lions that he isn't paying any attention at all to the briefcase. You bend over as though you are tying your shoe. When you get up, you pick the briefcase up and turn in the other direction.

You make it ten steps before a security guard yells, "Hey, kid! Put down that briefcase!" The guard is walking toward you quickly.

You freeze. Should you run?

"Hold it there, kid!" the guard says.

"Hold on, sir," the man without the briefcase says. "I think I may be able to clear this up."

Before the man can continue, your grandpa comes out of the restaurant. "My briefcase!" he yells, rushing over to you and taking the briefcase from you. Grandma, Zelda, and George come out of the restaurant, too.

"Where has everyone gone to?" Grandma mutters, then she sees you and Grandpa with the briefcase.

Turn to page 61.

"Ready?" Mission Control asks you, months later.

You are floating in space above the Earth, the big blue marble. Even with all your time training, it still grabs your attention. Watching the clouds swirl and the dawn and sunset lines of light and dark march around the globe can draw you in for hours. Right now, though, you need to focus on your job.

You have to be careful with each of your movements. If you drop a nut or bolt, it could rip through the solar panels, or hit something else. The garden module is gently floating towards the space station and you watch as the little jets go off to position it precisely.

Silently, the garden module and the space station come together. You lock the connectors into place, then crawl into the garden module. You are the only one with the right skills, and you can fit into the small spaces where the water and air lines are held.

Sweat dribbles down your face, and your hands ache from holding the tools through the clumsy fingers of the spacesuit. Finally, you turn the wrench and lock the last piece into place. You look down on the Earth again and smile.

The End

"The video we watched said it takes more than an hour to go through the whole Geo-Line area," you tell everyone. "We should go there first!"

Even Zelda agrees with you, so you head to the Geo-Line.

Getting dressed in the zip-line safety harness and helmet is tricky. You, George, and Zelda get help from the safety crew, but Grandma and Grandpa slip theirs on right away. Have they done this before?

"We'll have to skip the first few lines and go directly to the Deep River Gorge line to try and catch the man with the briefcase!" Grandma says brightly.

When you get to the platform, you look down and feel like the whole world has dropped away beneath you. You can see the river far below, and it looks like just a thin ribbon from up here.

"I'm not going! You can't make me!" George screams when you reach the platform.

Turn to page 44.

Your grandparents look at each other.

"Let's look for the man with the briefcase at the ice cream shop, George!" Grandpa says kindly.

"Is that the one where they send the ice cream to your table on mini-zip-lines?" George asks, forgetting how scared he was a moment ago. They walk away, and you wish you were going with them. Zelda looks down at you and smiles.

"Come on Goof-face, let's do this!" she says.

Grandma rides the zip-line first. She hops on the line without any help, puts her gloved hand on the cable, adjusts her goggles, gives a whoop, and drops away from the platform in the blink of an eye. Zelda goes next, and then it is your turn.

You look down again and feel queasy when the safety attendant attaches your harness to the line. Before you have time to think about it, the attendant reminds you to use your hand to brake, but not too much (or you'll get stuck in the middle!), and pushes you off the edge of the platform.

Turn to page 48.

The co-pilot helps all five of you strap into the seats in the escape pod. This time you are buckled in with ten belts. Your face is right next to George's.

"Your breath stinks!" he says, wrinkling his nose.

"Yours too, monkey-mouth," you say, trying not to sound scared.

The co-pilot closes the door to the escape pod and it shuts with such a loud clunk that you can feel the vibration over that of the plane.

Turn to page 47.

BANG!

You tumble and spin in the escape pod as it is launched from the plane. The spinning continues for what feels like a long time before the pod's parachutes open. You are glad you are strapped in so tightly as you lurch against your safety belts.

After that, the ride down is almost pleasant as the parachutes slow you down. You see the ground rush at you through the tiny window on your right.

BAM!

You hit the ground, and everyone in the pod lets out a yell. You've landed safely in a field within sight of the Space Center, and you see an SUV is already headed your way to collect you.

"We made it," says Grandma, giving you a big smile.

"Can we do it again?" George asks, struggling to unbuckle himself.

"Not today," Grandpa says with a laugh.

The End

You feel like you are flying! The wind in your face carries away your shout of joy. All of your fear is gone. You zip through a cloud, and your face gets wet. How will you know when to stop? Before you can worry too much, you come out on the other side of the cloud into bright sunshine. The walls of the gorge are approaching fast! The rock wall is a dark red and you start braking when you get into the shadow made by the cliff above.

You come screaming into the platform, and the park workers have to use the foam stopper to keep you from knocking into people. Zelda and Grandma give you high fives anyway.

"So, there is an optional rope-belay and rock climb here, but we think we should keep going to try and catch up with the man with the briefcase," Zelda says bossily, not giving you a chance to say what you think. You are still so excited from the ride that you don't mind.

Turn to page 50.

Zelda goes first on the next zip-line, followed by Grandma, who rides superhero-style. You are about to get on the zip-line when you see a man climb up the rock-climbing wall and onto the platform. He is wearing a helmet, but you can still see his blond hair and scar on his cheek! It must be the man with the briefcase.

He talks to the attendants on the platform for a second then climbs away on a ladder that stretches into the sky.

"You going or not?" an attendant with a sparse mustache asks, shaking your harness a little. What should you do? Maybe you should go after Grandma and Zelda and tell them that you found the man with the briefcase, but then he could get away!

If you choose to climb the ladder to see where the man with the briefcase has gone, turn to page 56.

If you decide that it is better to go find your grandma and Zelda than to go after the man alone, turn to page 59.

"Get ready for top speed!" the captain says.

The plane jumps forward, and you are glad you are strapped in so tightly. At first, top speed is exciting, but then it gets a little boring.

"I'm thirsty," George whines. "I don't like the bumpy air!"

"Sorry, buddy," Grandpa tells him. "The air turbulence will be over soon, but there are no drinks on the Vomit Comet."

"Not funny," George tells him. "I'm hungry too."

"We'll get you something when we get back, sweetie," Grandma tells him. You are also hungry and thirsty, but you don't say anything.

After an hour, the plane dives through patchy clouds and you see the blue ocean below you. Up ahead is the island, and there is a huge tower of dark smoke coming up from it. It does not look like there is any place to land. The cloud of smoke gets closer, and you fly right through it!

On the other side of the cloud of smoke is a small area of the runway that is not on fire. *WHAM!*

Turn to page 54.

You land so hard your teeth snap against each other, but you don't bite your tongue. You look around and see that the rest of your family is okay. As soon as you come to a stop, the co-pilot rushes to the door and swings it open. He lowers a red rope ladder out the door and scrambles down it.

"Thank you for getting us!" a woman says to you as she boards. Her face is smudged and her hair is wild. Eight more people climb into the plane, and it becomes hot and smoky inside. Outside the window, you can see the fire getting closer. The co-pilot helps direct the plane to turn it around from outside.

Finally he climbs aboard and closes the door.

"Hold on, folks!" the captain says. The other passengers grab anything they can because there are not enough seats. You can see the ocean right beneath you as the plane takes off.

You are thirstier than you have ever been in your whole life by the time you land at the Space Center. Claire, the director of the Space Center, rushes to greet you.

Go on to the next page.

"Thank you for your bravery!" Claire says to your family. "You are true heroes. I would want you on my space crew any day."

"I wasn't scared!" George says, taking a break from guzzling an energy drink.

"Of course you weren't, dear," Grandma says with a laugh.

"The director is right, you three have proven yourselves today," Grandpa says. "Grandma and I would definitely take you on any future missions."

The End

This might be your only chance to catch the man with the scar. You think you should take the ladder and follow him.

"Where does the ladder go?" you ask the attendant.

"It goes up to the Geology Learning Center and View Platform, at the edge of the gorge."

"Thanks!"

The ladder climb is scarier than zip-lining. It goes up and up, and you get tired well before you reach the top. You are sweating through your gear, but you don't care. You must find the man with the briefcase.

You race to the View Platform. It is built carefully into the side of the cliff. There are big rental binoculars mounted into the floor along the edge, and the Learning Center is behind it, higher on the cliff.

There he is! You see the blond man looking through the last pair of binoculars on the left. You creep closer, trying to act cool, as if you were just taking a look at the view, and use your own money to pay for the set of binoculars next to his.

Turn to page 58.

Staring at the man's cheek as he presses his eyes against the binoculars, you see his scar is gone.

"What happened to your scar?" you blurt out.

"What?" the man asks, looking at you.

"On your cheek, you had a scar before!"

"Oh," the man says, laughing and rubbing his cheek. "That was just red mud from the climb, I washed most of it off in the bathroom."

By the time you find your grandparents and brother and sister, everyone is really worried.

"Never run off like that!" they say. You don't tell them that you didn't "run off," but actually "climbed away."

The End

You decide you should follow your grandma and Zelda.

"I'm going," you tell the attendant holding your harness, and hop onto the zip-line.

This zip-line is different from the first. It is flatter and goes along the side of the gorge. The guy with the mustache said not to brake, but you don't want to crash, so you brake just a little. The ride is beautiful and you look down, up and all around as you fly through the air. You are a few hundred yards away from the platform when you slow down and come to a complete stop.

You're stuck!

You shout to your grandma and Zelda, but they can't hear you and just wave. Even though you know you are safe, hanging in the air high up is scary. An attendant climbs out and brings you back.

It takes a long time before she pulls you to the platform. You tell your grandma and Zelda what you saw, but by the time someone is able to check it out, the man with the briefcase is gone.

The End

You can't be *sure* that it is the right briefcase. The man with the scar is scary.

You hurry back to the table. George is cuddling with his stuffed animal.

"Come with me," you tell your family. "I saw the 'target,' the man with the briefcase. He's just outside!"

"Dear, you get the bill, and I'll go *see* about this briefcase!" Grandma says, grabbing your hand and marching to the door. "Walk as quickly as you can," she says, "but try not to draw attention to yourself."

The blond man with the scar is still taking pictures of the lions, but he turns around and looks directly at you and Grandma. He gives a start and then grabs the briefcase and runs away.

"Get that man!" Grandma yells. Grandpa comes out of the restaurant and runs after the man with the briefcase, but he has too much of a head start, and he disappears around the corner.

Turn to page 73.

"As I was saying," the blond man with the scar says, "I may be able to resolve this problem."

"This is my briefcase of very valuable items! You stole it at this very park, last week," Grandpa says.

"I'm sorry about that," the man says. "I have the *exact* same briefcase and I absentmindedly picked it up. I realized I had taken someone else's briefcase by mistake. I came back today to turn it in to the lost and found, but I was distracted by the mountain lions! Please take it, and again, I am sorry."

"Well, okay," Grandpa says, squinting at him.

"Thank you, young man," Grandma says.

The guard gives a nervous laugh and says, "I guess everything's okay then?"

The rest of the day is amazing. You have a great time. By the end you are so tired that your grandparents have to carry you to the car.

"Grandma?" you ask sleepily. "What is in the briefcase that is so valuable? Is it jewels?"

"Oh, no, dear!" Grandma says, patting your cheek. "Something more important than jewels."

Turn to page 67.

You decide you want to visit the underwater simulator first. Benedict takes you to the underwater training pool. Putting on the bulky spacesuit is hard. Two people help you step into the pool.

At first it is scary being underwater, but soon you can barely even tell the water is there.

"I'm flying in space," George says, sticking out his arms and legs.

You explore the pool. There are different training workstations with tools and instructions. You start with the easiest one, where you need to tighten a screw onto a plate of metal. It only takes you one try. Without even thinking about it, you speed through the next five training stations.

Zelda and George left the pool a long time ago, but you feel completely comfortable. Your breathing is steady, and you move through the water more easily than you do on land. When you climb out of the pool, you see the director, Claire, talking to your grandparents and a group of people in lab coats holding tablets.

"Can I talk to you?" Claire asks.

"Sure," you say, looking around.

Turn to the next page.

"I'll get right to the point," Claire says, looking directly at you. "You remind me of your grandparents. They have always done incredible work on every job. From the jungles to the South Pole, they have accepted every mission."

"Really? *My* grandparents?" you say, looking at Grandpa. He shrugs his shoulders and smiles.

"Yes, really," Claire says. "We want to offer you a job. We need help installing the garden module at the space station. But there's also another choice. We have just discovered an underwater city in the deep sea built so long ago that no one knows what it could be. The team is in desperate need of help installing the cameras and equipment they will use to find out."

"What about my family?" you ask.

"They could go with you," she says. "Think about it, ask your parents, and let me know. We need to make a decision soon."

If you decide to go to the space station, turn to page 40.

If you choose to explore the underwater city, turn to page 68.

The man with the briefcase gets tangled in his trench coat and falls down. Grandpa rushes to him and grabs the man's hands. "Get security!" Grandpa yells.

As you get closer to Grandpa and the blond man, the monkey Grandma was talking to before leaps through the air and grabs the briefcase.

"Good job, Suzy! You'll get extra bananas tonight," Grandma says, taking the briefcase from Suzy and giving her a gentle rub on the head.

Security arrives and takes control of the man with the scar. He doesn't fight, but he won't say anything. You wait for the police. Zelda takes lots of pictures.

"What's in the briefcase, Grandma?" you ask.

Turn to the next page.

"That briefcase has the top secret plans for the next project here at Mega Zip-Line Nature Exploration Park, and he works for their top competitor."

"But how did you know about it? How did you get Suzy to help?"

"Well," Grandma says, smiling, "there are lots of things you don't know about Grandpa and me! One of them is that I used to volunteer at the local zoo until they had to close it. Suzy and I are old friends. She is one smart cookie.

"Another thing you don't know is that we used to be top counter-espionage agents to make sure people weren't stealing secrets from our employers. We came out of retirement for this job because an old friend asked us to."

"How come Mom and Dad never told us about that?" you ask.

"Well, there are lots of things your parents don't know, either," Grandma says. "Let's go see the baby goats."

The End

"Inside of this briefcase, I keep all of the love letters your grandfather and I wrote to each other when we were young and in different parts of the world."

"Yucky, love letters are mushy!" George says, waking up a little. Everyone laughs so hard that Zelda takes off her headphones and asks, "What's so funny?"

The End

68

You and your family head to the South Pacific, where you train for the deep dive to the underwater city.

You wiggle your feet in the warm sand and look at the blue ocean, taking a break with your mom.

You have been training to put the sand vacuum in the main square of the city. So far you have had to practice in shallow water. Tomorrow you get to go out to the dig site. You are excited and nervous.

"Don't worry, we'll be there," Grandma says.

The next morning as you ride the speedboat out to the site, Grandma pulls you aside.

"We need to let you know something," she says, speaking directly into your ear.

"That you and Grandpa were spies and used to go on dangerous missions all over the world," you answer. "And that the trip to the Space Center was a test that you set up. Zelda, George, and I figured that out a long time ago."

Grandma looks surprised for a moment. "Well, that too, I guess. But I wanted to let you know that we think that the underwater site may have been built by aliens."

Turn to page 71.

"Wow!" you say, not sure if Grandma is joking.

"We thought you should know. Be very brave!"

Only an hour later, you are suited up in a high-pressure dive suit floating down into the darkness of the deep ocean. It feels like you fall for hours, but the timer says it only takes you nineteen minutes. Everything is greenish and your headlamp fades into black as you look out into the depths.

Below you, you finally see something. You look over to your teammates. "Okay, here we go," you say to the others through your helmet.

You come to the bottom, and you see graceful arches and spires all around you. The tops are covered in barnacles, corals, and other underwater growths. Below that, where the sand has been cleared, they are smooth and glint like liquid silver.

"Wow!" you say. You can't believe that you are here in an alien city underneath the ocean.

"Not the moon, but pretty cool," says Grandpa.

You grin and say, "I guess it's okay."

Grandma laughs.

You start to explore the city and get to work.

The End

"He's getting away!" Grandma says and then gives a piercing finger whistle.

You don't know why Grandma is whistling, so you follow the man with the briefcase—fast!

Turn to page 65.

ABOUT THE AUTHOR

After graduating from Williams College with a degree specialization in Ancient History, **Anson Montgomery** spent ten years founding and working in technology-related companies, as well as working as a freelance journalist for financial and local publications. He is the author of a number of books in the original *Choose Your Own Adventure* series, including *Everest Adventure, Snowboard Racer, Moon Quest* (reissued in 2008 by Chooseco), and *CyberHacker* as well as two volumes of *Choose Your Own Adventure — The Golden Path,* part of a three volume series. Anson lives in Warren, Vermont with his wife, Rebecca, and his two daughters, Avery and Lila.

ABOUT THE ILLUSTRATOR

Keith Newton began his art career in the theater as a set painter. Having talent and a strong desire to paint portraits, he moved to New York and studied fine art at the Art Students League. Keith has won numerous awards in art such as The Grumbacher Gold Medallion and Salmagundi Award for Pastel. He soon began illustrating and was hired by Disney Feature Animation where he worked on such films as *Pocahontas* and *Mulan* as a background artist. Keith also designed color models for sculptures at Disney Animal Kingdom and has animated commercials for Euro Disney. Today, Keith Newton freelances from his home and teaches entertainment illustration at The College for Creative Studies in Detroit. He is married and has two daughters.

For games, activities and other fun stuff, or to write to Anson Montgomery, visit us online at www.cyoa.com